George Brown, CLASS CLOWN

Help! I'm Stuck in a Giant Nostril!

For Amy and Jeff, just because—NK

For my father-in-law, Ken the Nose—AB

GROSSET & DUNLAP
Published by the Penguin Group
Penguin Group (USA) Inc., 375 Hudson Street, New York,
New York 10014, USA
Penguin Group (Canada), 90 Eglinton Avenue East, Suite 700,
Toronto, Ontario M4P 2Y3, Canada
(a division of Pearson Penguin Canada Inc.)
Penguin Books Ltd., 80 Strand, London WC2R 0RL, England
Penguin Group Ireland, 25 St. Stephen's Green, Dublin 2, Ireland
(a division of Penguin Books Ltd.)
Penguin Group (Australia), 250 Camberwell Road, Camberwell,
Victoria 3124, Australia
(a division of Pearson Australia Group Pty. Ltd.)
Penguin Books India Pvt. Ltd., 11 Community Centre, Panchsheel Park,
New Delhi—110 017, India
Penguin Group (NZ), 67 Apollo Drive, Rosedale,
Auckland 0632, New Zealand
(a division of Pearson New Zealand Ltd.)
Penguin Books (South Africa) (Pty.) Ltd., 24 Sturdee Avenue,
Rosebank, Johannesburg 2196, South Africa

Penguin Books Ltd., Registered Offices:
80 Strand, London WC2R 0RL, England

If you purchased this book without a cover, you should be aware that this
book is stolen property. It was reported as "unsold and destroyed" to the
publisher, and neither the author nor the publisher has received any payment
for this "stripped book."

The scanning, uploading, and distribution of this book via the Internet or via
any other means without the permission of the publisher is illegal and punishable
by law. Please purchase only authorized electronic editions and do not participate
in or encourage electronic piracy of copyrighted materials. Your support of
the author's rights is appreciated.

The publisher does not have any control over and does not assume any
responsibility for author or third-party websites or their content.

Text copyright © 2011 by Nancy Krulik. Illustrations copyright © 2011
by Aaron Blecha. All rights reserved. Published by Grosset & Dunlap,
a division of Penguin Young Readers Group, 345 Hudson Street,
New York, New York 10014. GROSSET & DUNLAP is a trademark of
Penguin Group (USA) Inc. Printed in the U.S.A.

Library of Congress Control Number: 2011000845

ISBN 978-0-448-45574-7   10 9 8 7 6 5 4 3 2

George Brown, CLASS CLOWN

Help! I'm Stuck in a Giant Nostril!

by Nancy Krulik

illustrated by Aaron Blecha

Grosset & Dunlap
An Imprint of Penguin Group (USA) Inc.

Chapter 1

"You will not burp! You will not burp!"

The whole time George Brown was asleep, his best friend **Alex's voice kept ringing in his ears.** Alex had slept over and right before the boys went to bed, Alex had recorded the message on George's MP3 player.

"You will not burp. You will not burp."

Rrrring! George's alarm clock went off. It was time to get up for school.

"Turn it off . . . too loud," Alex grumbled. He buried his head under his pillow.

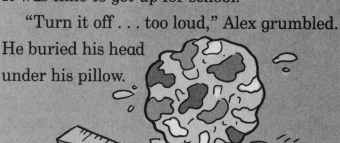

George hit the snooze button and rolled over. He *never* got up the first time the alarm clock rang.

Snore. George's nose buzzed.

"You will not burp. You will not burp," Alex's voice repeated over and over.

Rrrring! **The alarm clock sounded** again.

"Boys, are you up?" George's mother shouted from downstairs.

"Yes, ma'am," Alex called back to her. He sat up in his bed and rubbed his eyes.

Okay, now George *really* had to get up. He kicked off the covers and took off the headphones.

"How do you feel?" Alex asked him. "Any **bubbles** in your belly?"

George looked at Alex in the cot that was across the room. George wasn't usually allowed to have **sleepovers on school nights**, but Alex's parents had gone out of town. It was almost like having a brother—for one night, anyway. George sat very still and waited for his tummy to start rumbling.

"Nope," George said happily. "All quiet down there."

"That's a good sign," Alex said. "When I read in that science magazine about **planting ideas in people's heads** while they were sleeping, I figured maybe it would work on your burps."

George frowned when Alex said the word *burp*. George had wanted to keep his burping a secret. But Alex was smart. He'd figured out that George was hiding something. Something really, really awful—**a magical super burp**.

Alex was good at keeping secrets, so he was still the only person besides George who knew about George's problem. And lucky for George, Alex liked solving problems. The super burp was the worst thing that had happened to him since he'd moved to Beaver Brook. It was the worst thing in his whole life.

It all started on George's first day at Edith B. Sugarman Elementary School. George's dad was in the army, and his family moved around a lot. So there always seemed to be some new school where he was **the new kid**.

But this time, George had promised himself that things were going to be different. He was turning over a new leaf.

No more pranks. No more class clown. He wasn't going to get into any trouble anymore, like he had at all his old schools. He was going to raise his hand before he spoke. And he wasn't going to make funny faces or goof on his teachers behind their backs.

That last promise had been really hard for George to keep. Especially because his teacher, Mrs. Kelly, looked a little like a totem pole and did weird things like yodel and dance **the hula** right in the middle of class.

At the end of his first day, George had managed to stay out of trouble. Not only had he not been sent to the principal's office, he didn't even know who the principal was!

But you didn't have to be a math whiz like Alex to figure out how many friends being a well-behaved, not-so-funny kid will get you. Zero. Zilch. *None.*

That night, George's parents took him out to Ernie's Ice Cream Emporium. While they were sitting outside and George was finishing his root beer float, a shooting star flashed across the sky. So **George made a wish**.

I want to make kids laugh—but not get into trouble.

Unfortunately, **the star was gone** before George could finish the wish. So only half came true—the first half.

A minute later, George had a funny feeling in his belly. It was like there were hundreds of tiny bubbles bouncing around in there. The bubbles bounced up and down and all around. They **ping-ponged** their way into his chest and **bing-bonged** their way up into his throat. And then . . .

George let out a big burp. A *huge* burp. A SUPER burp!

The super burp was loud, and it was *magic*.

Suddenly George lost control of his

arms and legs.
It was like they
had minds of
their own. His
hands grabbed
straws and stuck
them up his nose
like a walrus. His
feet jumped up
on the table and
started dancing
the **hokey pokey**.
Everyone at Ernie's

Ice Cream Emporium started laughing—
except George's parents, who were covered
in ice cream from the sundaes he had
knocked over.

The magical super burps came back lots
of times after that. And every time a burp
came, it brought trouble with it. Like the
time it forced him to juggle raw eggs in his

classroom (which wouldn't have been so
bad if George knew *how* to juggle).

Or the time he'd burped in the middle
of a toy store and knocked down a whole
display of paddle ball games—right in
the window. A big crowd gathered around
just in time to see him get **kicked out** of
the store!

And who could forget the school talent show? The super burp burst out right in the middle of George's performance. It made him **dive-bomb off the stage**—and into the principal's lap! George definitely knew the principal now. He'd spent a whole lot of time sitting in her office after that one.

Most of the people at Edith B. Sugarman Elementary School just thought George was **clowning around** all the time. Only Alex knew the truth. And he wanted to help.

"Boys, it's **oh-seven hundred hours**," George's dad called from the kitchen. "Better get a move on. Chow's almost ready."

Alex gave George a funny look. "What did he say?"

George laughed. "That's army talk for 'it's seven o'clock, and you'd better hurry because breakfast is almost ready.'"

"Great, and remember," Alex said as they finished getting dressed, "you will not burp. **You will not burp.** You will not burp."

Chapter 2

"I've never had waffles shaped like spaceships before," Alex told George. The boys were sitting in the kitchen while George's parents got ready for work.

"My dad gets them at the PX," George said.

"What's a PX?" Alex asked.

"It's a giant store on the army base," George said. "They have everything." He poured some maple syrup on his waffles.

George was about to take a bite. But before he could open his mouth, he felt **something weird and wild** bubbling around in his belly.

Oh no! Could the super burp be back?

George shut his mouth tight and tried to keep the burp from slipping out.

But the super burp wasn't going to be stopped by two little lips. Already it was bing-bonging its way around George's kidneys and ping-ponging over his liver. Then it zigzagged around George's teeth and . . .

George let out a killer burp! It was so loud an alien in outer space could have heard it on his spaceship.

"Oh no!" Alex groaned. "Not again."

Yes, again. **The super burp was out, and it really wanted to play.** Before George knew what was happening, his hands grabbed one of the waffles.

"Heads up!" George's mouth shouted. Then his hands flung the waffle across the table like it was a Frisbee.

Alex ducked. The waffle missed his head. But **a glob of syrup** landed right in the middle of his forehead.

The waffle hit the wall. Ooey, gooey maple syrup splattered all over the place.

"Dude!" Alex shouted. "What are you doing?"

George wasn't doing anything. The super burp was in charge now. It was as if George was an old-fashioned puppet and the burp was pulling his strings.

"Incoming spaceship!" George's mouth shouted as his hands grabbed the waffle from Alex's plate and winged it across the room.

"Boys?" George's mom called from the other room. **"What's going on in there?"**

"N-n-nothing," Alex called back quickly. Then he whispered to George, "Cut it out."

But George *couldn't* cut it out. His hands reached out and grabbed two forks. Then they started playing the drums on the glasses and the plates.

Clink. Clank. Clink. Clank. Crash!

Oops. One of the plates fell off the table and broke into about a gazillion pieces.

"George, did you remember to brush your teeth?" his mom called from the other room.

"Yeah!" George's mouth shouted back. "But I forgot to gargle!" And with that he grabbed a glass of orange juice and poured it into his mouth. Then he gargled the juice straight up into the air—**like a giant George juice fountain**.

Whoosh! Suddenly George felt something pop in the bottom of his belly. It was like someone had punctured a balloon. **All the air rushed out of him.** The super burp was gone.

But George was still there. And so was the giant mess the super burp had left. There were waffles, syrup, juice, and pieces of the cracked plate all over the kitchen. Alex wiped the glob of syrup off his face and

looked around. "That was a bad one," he said quietly.

George nodded.

"What happened in here?" George's dad asked as he walked into the kitchen. He looked mad.

George didn't know how to answer. He couldn't just say that a super burp made him fling waffles, break a plate, and gargle orange juice.

Alex didn't say anything, either. He looked too scared to even talk.

Besides, George's dad didn't wait for an answer. He handed George a sponge and gave Alex a mop.

"You two are on KP duty," George's dad told the boys. Then he turned and stormed out of the room.

"That means cleanup duty," George told Alex.

"I figured," Alex said. He started swishing the mop around the floor.

"Sorry about this," George said as he wiped some syrup from the wall. "It's the stupid super burp."

"I know," Alex said. "I really hoped that MP3 thing would work. It seemed so simple."

George frowned. Maybe that was the problem. It was going to take something a lot tougher than an MP3 player to squelch that belch once and for all.

"Well, look on the bright side," Alex said.

George gave him a strange look. "*What* bright side?"

"You've already burped," Alex explained. "So maybe you'll be **burp-free** the rest of the day."

George could only hope Alex was right. Because burping at home was a pain in the neck. But burping at school was just plain embarrassing!

Chapter 3

"My nosey nose smells stinky feet. My tingly tongue tastes something sweet!" Mrs. Kelly sang as she strummed a weird, squeaky instrument called a zither. It was kind of like a cross between a guitar and a shoe box. "Ouch! Don't touch a stove that's hot. My eyes can see a leopard's spot. Ask me what my ears can do. They hear **a five-senses boogaloo**."

Mrs. Kelly picked up her zither and started dancing around the room while singing her song.

Mrs. Kelly sure was making it hard to be the new and improved George today. His teacher's singing voice was so bad, it would make a dog howl. And as she passed by, her perfume stunk so much, it would make an elephant fold up its trunk and leave. But he didn't say that. He didn't say *anything*.

"That's a special song I wrote about the five senses," Mrs. Kelly told the class as she finished strumming. **"Smell, taste, touch, hearing, and sight."**

Now this was a subject George knew a lot about. So he raised his hand—like a good George should. Mrs. Kelly gave him one of her big, gummy smiles.

"Yes, George," she said.

"Humans aren't the only ones with senses," he said. "I work at Mr. Furstman's pet store sometimes, and I'm learning a lot about animals.

Like, did you know that scientists think that parrots' eyes are so sensitive that they can see more colors than humans can? Or that hamsters like to taste their food before they eat it? And if they don't like it, they'll spit it out?"

Mrs. Kelly gave George an even bigger grin. Now he could see every one of her big teeth. Yellow stuff was stuck between them. Maybe she'd had eggs for breakfast. "That's excellent, George.

Animals do have very strong senses. Like my cat, Fester. She's a finicky eater, too. But that's because cats have fewer taste buds than we humans do."

"My brother, Sam, will eat anything," Louie volunteered. "One time he even ate snails. His taste buds are **very sophisticated**."

"Sam's a great eater," Louie's friend Max said. "I saw him eat once."

"Yeah," Louie's other friend, Mike, added. "Sam can really pig out."

Louie shot Mike a dirty look.

"I mean in a good way," Mike added quickly.

Mrs. Kelly smiled at the class. "We're going to learn all about the five senses up close and personal," she told them. "We're going on a field trip tomorrow!"

"Ooh!" Julianna exclaimed. "Are we going to **the Human Room-In**?"

"Yes, we are!" Mrs. Kelly exclaimed excitedly. "The whole fourth grade is going to the Beaver Brook Science Center to see their special exhibit on the five senses."

"I've been to the Human Room-In," Julianna told the class. "It's really cool. There's a giant trampoline that looks like a big, red tongue."

Wow! George was really excited now. **This sounded cool!**

"My brother, Sam, and I have been to the Beaver Brook Science Center a gazillion times," Louie said. "We have special passes."

George looked over at Alex. **"Here he goes again,"** he whispered. "Brag, brag, brag."

"George, do you have something to add?" Mrs. Kelly asked him.

Oops. George had almost forgotten to be new and improved. "No. I was just saying that having to wait until

tomorrow is a drag, drag, drag."

Phew. Good save.

"We're all excited," Mrs. Kelly agreed. She gave Louie a gummy smile. "Did you want to tell us something else about the science center?" she asked him.

"We have to make a stop in my new room," Louie told her. "My family gave **a ton of money** to the museum, so they named a room after us."

The kids all looked at him strangely. Who had their own room in a museum?

"It's the Farley Family Fungus Room," Louie explained. "My dad once had **a really bad case of athlete's foot**. His feet got all crackly and red. Finally, this one doctor, Dr. Pedis, got rid of it for him. So my dad donated this money so people could find out more about fungi."

"We'll definitely go in that room, Louie," Mrs. Kelly said. "I can't wait to see what fungi they've found."

"It's *full* of fungi," Louie assured her.

Louie was bragging again, although

having your own room in a museum was pretty cool. But it wasn't a surprise. Louie was rich. He had lots of things no one else had. And he always made sure everybody knew about them.

That was another way George and Louie were different. **George had something no one else had, too.** Only he never bragged. A burp was something you just

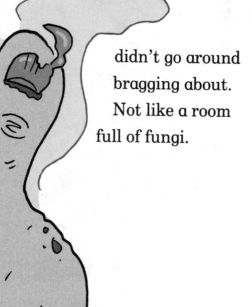

didn't go around bragging about. Not like a room full of fungi.

Chapter 4

"Dude, I can't believe you're going to eat that spaghetti," George said to his friend Chris as they sat with the other fourth-graders during lunch.

"I like spaghetti," Chris told him.

"Me too," George said. "But it's all mushy and covered in gunk."

"It's okay," Chris said. "I don't have to chew as much this way."

George looked at the spaghetti in tomato sauce on his lunch tray. A part of him wanted to shove strands of saucy spaghetti up his nose and let them hang down. They would look like **the world's longest bloody boogers**. That would have cracked up the kids in his old school.

But that was then. This was now. And George wasn't going to stick stuff up his nose anymore. He started eating his canned peaches instead.

"This field trip sounds awesome," Alex said. "The last time I went to the science museum I got to slice up a cow eyeball. It was the size of a Ping-Pong ball."

"**At my old school**, we once went to a natural history museum and someone yanked a bone out of this giant dinosaur and the whole thing collapsed. *Boom!* The guy who worked there burst out crying. It was even in the newspaper!"

Sage shot George a goofy smile and batted her eyelashes up and down. "That sounds like the coolest field trip ever, **Georgie**," she said.

George felt like he was going to puke up his peaches. Why did Sage have to call him that?

Louie overheard George. He poked him in the back. "So what if you went to see some dumb dinosaur on a dumb old field trip from your dumb old school," he said. "Wait until you see the giant mushrooms in the Farley Family Fungus Room. You can look through a microscope and see athlete's foot fungus up close. It's disgusting!"

POKE

"Foot fungus is way cooler than a dinosaur bone," Mike said.

"Yeah, you should see the fungus on my dad's big toe," Max added. "Even at the beach my mom makes him wear socks so she doesn't have to look at it."

George ignored Louie and the Echoes. "You guys want to hang out after school today?" he asked Alex, Chris, and Julianna. "We can go to my house. We can take turns on my skateboard."

"My brother, Sam, bought a superdeluxe skateboard," Louie told George. "It cost two hundred dollars. He did this new trick where he popped way up in the air. Of course, he can only go on it when he's not at baseball practice. You should see him play baseball. He's—"

"We know. We know.

The Yankees can't wait to sign him." George interrupted Louie. Everybody in the fourth grade heard about Sam all the time. How he was president of his class in middle school and how he was captain of the soccer and basketball teams.

"Sam, Sam, Sam," George said to him. "I bet you can't go a whole day without talking about your big brother."

Everyone stopped and stared at George.

"Whoa," Mike and Max said at once.

"Oh yeah?" Louie said. "Well, uh, well . . ."
Louie seemed stumped for a minute. But
then he said, "I bet you can't go a whole
day without talking about your old school."

"Sure, I can," George said. "No problem."

Louie smiled. "Good, **then it's a bet**."

Mike looked at him. "What are you
betting?" he asked Louie.

Louie thought for a minute. Then a
creepy smiled spread across his face.
"Whoever loses has to be **the winner's
servant** for a whole day."

"Yeah?" George said. "My mother's been bugging me to clean my room. So *when* you are my servant for the day, be sure to bring dust rags and a broom."

"It'll never happen," Louie told him. "You're going down, Brown."

"Yeah?" George said. "Well, Farley, you're going . . ." George stopped. He couldn't think of anything that rhymed with Farley except barley. That didn't sound bad enough. "You're going to lose," he said finally.

Chapter 5

"Why did you make that bet with Louie?" Julianna asked George that afternoon after school. She, Chris, and Alex were all hanging out on George's front porch. "If you lose, he's going to make you miserable."

George popped a piece of cinnamon gum in his mouth and grinned. "I'm not going to lose the bet," he told Julianna.

"Louie will talk about Sam way before
I talk about **my old you-know-what**. He
can't help himself."

Chris popped a cinnamon gum bubble.
"Louie brags about Sam a lot," he said.

"He brags about *everything*." George
shoved another three sticks of gum in his
mouth and started to chew. Red drool spit

out of the corner of his mouth. It looked
kind of like blood.

"Chew the gum really, really well
before we add it to the ABC gum ball,"
Alex told the other kids. "It needs to be
sticky. Otherwise it falls off."

Alex was trying to break the record
for the biggest already been chewed gum

ball so he could get in the *Schminess Book of World Records*. All his friends were helping him.

George pulled his wad of chewed-up gum out of his mouth and handed it to Alex. Then he grabbed his skateboard and helmet. **"You guys ready to ride?"** he asked.

"Sure!" Julianna said.

"Are you going to show me how to do a 360 kick flip today?" Chris asked. "You said you would."

"Definitely," George agreed. "It's not that hard." He picked up his skateboard and walked to his driveway. He noticed that his dad had raked up all the leaves in the front yard. There were huge piles everywhere.

George put his skateboard down and snapped on his helmet. The driveway went downhill, and the cement was nice and smooth. **It was a pretty good place to do a 360.**

"Okay, so to do a 360 kick flip," he told his friends, "you put your front foot just

behind the front truck bolt on the board. Then as you move, begin to wind your body a little bit, so when you go in the air you are ready to spin—"

Suddenly, George stopped talking. **Something weird was spinning inside him.** *Something awful.* And it was all George could think about.

Bubble. Bubble. **George was in trouble.**

The super burp had stayed inside all through the school day. But now it wanted to come out and play.

George shut his mouth tight. He pushed really hard on his stomach. **He just had to squelch this belch!**

But the burp was strong. Really strong. Already it had bing-bonged its way out of his stomach and ping-ponged its way up into his throat. *Bing-bong. Ping-pong. Bing-bong.*

George let out a burp. A **superpowered**, 360-degree mega burp. It was so loud, it shook the leaves right off the trees!

"Uh-oh . . . ," Alex said
with a gulp. He raced
after George and tried to
tackle him.

But Alex was no match for the
super burp.

Oomph. Alex fell face-first on the
front lawn.

George's legs bent at the knees. His
skateboard sprung up off the ground.

"Cowabunga!" George shouted as he ollied through the air and landed in the biggest pile of leaves.

Red, yellow, and orange leaves flew everywhere. Then he headed for the second-biggest pile. Chris and Julianna ran up onto the lawn.

"Your dad is going to kill you!" Julianna shouted.

But the super burp didn't care what kind of trouble George was going to be in. Burps just want to have fun!

George's hands grabbed bunches of leaves and started shoving them down his pants and up his sweater. He stuck a leaf up his nose and another in his ear.

"You look like a scarecrow!" Chris laughed really hard.

That was all George's ears had to hear. He stuck his arms straight out like a scarecrow. Then his mouth began shouting really loudly. "Boo! Are you scared crows? Boo!"

"Caw! Caw!"

At just that moment, two big, black crows flew by. They weren't scared by the George scarecrow at all. One of them landed on his head. The other perched on his arm.

"Caw! Caw!" the crow on George's head cried out.

"Caw! Caw!" George's mouth shouted back.

Now the crows were scared. They took off and flew away—but not before one of them left George a **special present**.

"Whoa!" Alex exclaimed. "Feel that slime dripping on your head? It's crow poop!"

Suddenly . . . *whooosh!* George felt something go pop in the bottom of his belly. It felt like the air had rushed right out of him.

The super burp was gone. **But George was still there**, with leaves stuck in his sweater and crow poop on his head.

Alex raced over to him. "I tried to stop you . . . really I did," he said.

George nodded. "It's not your fault." He looked around at the yard. "I gotta clean up this mess before my dad sees it." The words were barely out of his mouth when his dad pulled up in his car.

"George!" he shouted as he opened the front car door.

The kids all gulped.

"It took me two hours to rake those leaves," George's dad said. He was standing with his hands on his hips and shaking his head. "What happened?"

"It's all my fault, Dad," George said, even though it wasn't. **It was the burp's fault.** "I'm really sorry."

"George—*um*—was trying to be a scarecrow," Chris told him.

George could tell Chris was trying to help. But it wasn't working.

"Why would you want to do that?" George's dad asked.

"Um . . . to scare away crows?" Alex answered hopefully.

"He did it, too," Julianna said. "A couple of crows came by, but they flew off because they were really scared."

"See, Dad?" George asked, pointing to the bird poop on the top of his head.

"Well, George's job isn't to be a scarecrow," his dad said. He went into the garage and came back with a rake. "Your new job is to rake up all these leaves again."

"But, Dad," George pleaded. "I was just about to teach Chris how to do a 360 kick flip."

"Not today, you're not," George's dad told him. "Attention!"

George stood up straight.

"Now start raking," his dad ordered.

"Yes, sir," George said sadly. He started moving the rake around the lawn.

"We'll stay and help," Alex said.

George's dad shook his head. "George made the mess. He'll clean up the mess."

As George's friends walked off, waving sadly to him, George's dad frowned. "Sometimes I just don't know **what gets into you**, son," he said.

George didn't know what to tell him. After all, it wasn't what got into George that caused all the trouble. It was what burst *out* of him—big, troublemaking burps.

Chapter 6

Bump! Thump! Bump!

"Whoa." George rubbed his rear end as the school bus hit another pothole.

Alex groaned. "**It's like being on a bad roller coaster.** I hope we get to the museum soon."

"At my—" George was about to say how at his old school they took nice buses with seats that reclined and bathrooms in the back. But he stopped himself the minute he saw Louie staring at him.

"What were you going to say?" Louie asked him.

George shook his head. "**Nothing. I** wasn't going to say anything."

Louie frowned, which made George smile for the first time that day. He was in a rotten mood. It had taken him three hours to rake the leaves yesterday, and after that his dad had still made him do his regular chores like taking out all the trash. His arms and legs were really sore. **Yesterday's super burp had really been a pain.**

"What if I burp at the museum?" George said quietly to Alex.

"Maybe we should come up with a signal," Alex suggested. "So if you feel like the you-know-what is about to come out, I can grab you and take you into the bathroom or some other place where you can't get in any trouble. I'll stick close by you."

George wasn't sure there was any place where the super burp couldn't get him into trouble. But it was worth a try.

"How about you **tap your belly**?"
Alex suggested. "It always starts there,
anyway."

George nodded. A tap wasn't the kind
of thing that would look too weird to the
other kids. It might just work.

That made George feel a little better.
But he thought of something that would
make him feel *a lot* better.

"Hey, Louie," George called. "The museum sounds so cool. I know there are a lot of things for **us fourth-graders** to see. But what about older kids? What kind of stuff is there for them?"

"Are you kidding?" Louie asked. "My older bro—" He stopped himself in the middle of the word. "Nice try, George," he said. "But I'm not saying anything."

"Me either," George told him. "In fact, I'm not going to say another word until we get to the museum." And with that, **George zipped his lips**. It was a lot safer that way.

"Here we are!" Louie shouted excitedly as the kids walked into the exhibit. "The Farley Family Fungus Room!"

George looked to his left. There was **a huge sculpture of the entire Farley family**

next to the sign. For a minute, George thought about chewing up a piece of gum and sticking it in Louie's nose so it would look like snot. That would have been pretty funny. But it wasn't something a new and improved George would do. The new and improved George didn't want to

FARLEY
FAMILY
FUNGUS
ROOM

THE
FARLEYS

get into any trouble on this field trip.

George and Chris started to walk around the room. They stopped and stared at a big bathtub oozing with mold.

"That's a good reason to never take a bath," George pointed out.

"I bet there's **really nasty fungus** around a toilet bowl, too," Chris said. "Maybe I can put that into my next Toiletman comic. He could be fighting fungus in bathrooms across the world."

"Yeah," George said. "You could call it *Toiletman: Fighting a Fungus among Us!*"

The boys passed by a computer where

Sage and Julianna were playing Find the Fungus.

"What exactly is a fungus, anyway?" George asked Chris. "Is it some sort of plant?"

Chris shrugged. "I thought it was a type of animal."

Mrs. Kelly heard them talking. "Actually fungi aren't animals or plants. They're their own scientific family. Scientists have found at least seventy-five thousand different kinds of fungi. Mold is a fungus. So is yeast."

George looked around for some interesting fungi. But **all he saw were mushrooms**.

"Then why are these here?" George asked out loud. "Aren't mushrooms plants? Like vegetables?"

"Nope. Mushrooms are a kind of fungus," Louie told him. He sounded really proud that he knew that. "And these aren't just any mushrooms. These are some of the **most interesting** mushrooms in the world."

Interesting mushrooms? Those were two words that George didn't think belonged together. Why come all the way to the museum to see mushrooms? They could have stayed in the school cafeteria and taken a tour of the salad bar.

POISONOUS

Still, a few of the mushrooms were kind of cool. Especially the giant red one with the little, white blobs all over it.

"I wouldn't want that on my salad," George joked.

"You're not kidding," Alex told him. "According to what it says here, that's an amanita mushroom. It's poisonous. **Two bites could kill a grown man.**"

George put his hands around his throat, tipped his head back, and let his tongue flop out of the side of his mouth. He looked like a guy who'd just been poisoned.

"Hey, don't goof around," Louie said. "Fungi are serious business."

George laughed. **Louie could be such a weirdo.**

"Want to go watch the movie about the life cycle of the yellow brain fungus?" Chris asked George and Alex.

"If you and George want to," Alex said.

George shrugged. He couldn't imagine that a yellow-brained fungus had a very exciting life. So instead he walked over to a diorama where there were 3-D models of people's feet with round, red ringworm fungus. The skin looked all dry and scaly.

"Ringworm is an itchy fungus," Louie told him. "A lot of athletes get it because they walk around barefoot in the locker room and it gets into their feet."

George smiled. "Do you know any athletes who have had ringworm?" he asked **Louie**.

"Sure," Louie said. "Friends of my bro—" He stopped for a minute and shook his head. "Oh no! But you're not

getting me to say what you want me to say. I told you, **you're the one going down, Brown**."

Grrr. George almost had him that time.

Looking at the scaly ringworm feet made George feel **all itchy**. He reached down and scratched his belly.

Suddenly, Alex grabbed his arm and yanked him away from the other kids.

"Outta our way!" Alex said as he pulled George across the room.

"What are you doing?" George shouted.

"This is for your own good," Alex told George as he pushed him into the bathroom.

George rolled through the door and lay sprawled out on the tile floor. "Why are you doing this?" he asked Alex.

"To keep you out of trouble," Alex answered. He stopped and looked curiously at George. "Aren't you going to burp?"

"No," George said as he stood back up.

"But you scratched your belly," Alex told him.

"Because I felt itchy looking at the ringworm," George said. "Besides, the burp signal is *tapping* my belly, **not scratching it**."

"Oh yeah," Alex said. "It's kind of confusing. Sorry."

"How about I tap my belly and rub my head at the same time if I feel the super burp?" George suggested.

Suddenly there was a knock on the door. "Are you boys okay in there?" Mrs. Kelly asked.

Alex opened the door and walked out
with George.

"We're fine," Alex said. "Um—I just had
to go to the bathroom really bad. And you
said we weren't allowed to go anywhere
without a buddy. So I grabbed George."

"Oh," Mrs. Kelly said. **"That was very
responsible of you, Alex.** Now follow me,
boys. We're ready to go into the

Human Room-In. Unless you want to see some more fungi."

George thought about the moldy bathtub, the huge, red mushroom, and the funky feet with ringworm. "Nah. I'm good," he said.

"Me too," Alex said.

George whispered to him, "I'm never asking for mushrooms on pizza again."

NOW
LEAVING
THE
FARLEY
FAMILY
FUNGUS
ROOM

Chapter 7

Lub-dub. Lub-dub. Lub-dub.

The giant heart beat loudly in George's ears as he and the other kids filed one by one up the ramp of the giant heart and through the tricuspid valve.

"You are now traveling the route **real blood corpuscles** take when they go through the heart," a recording said.

"Corpuscle George Brown reporting for duty," George said. He raised his hand in a salute.

"At ease, corpuscle," Julianna said.

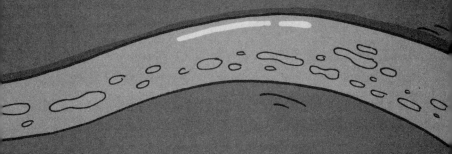

She was right in front of George. "See, I told you this was fun. And it only gets cooler."

Lub-dub. Lub-dub.

Julianna was right. But going through the heart was also a little scary—it was so dark and noisy. **George wondered if his blood got freaked out** every time it went through his heart. It was probably even darker and noisier inside his body. Not just the heartbeat. What about the super burp? It sounded so loud from the outside. He couldn't even imagine what it sounded like *inside*.

"Hey, Julianna," George said. "Do you know where vampires keep their money?"

"No, where?" Julianna called back to him.

"In a blood bank!" George started to laugh. That was a pretty good joke. Not a super burp kind of joke. **Just a normal kid joke.** The kind of joke George always liked to tell when he was a little nervous.

When George emerged from the giant tunnel that was the aorta, he found himself in a different room, **a room as big as the school gym**. It wasn't dark anymore. It was really bright. Kids were running around everywhere. Some were jumping

THE ARMPIT ARCHES

SNOT SLIDE

TONGUE TRAMPOLINE

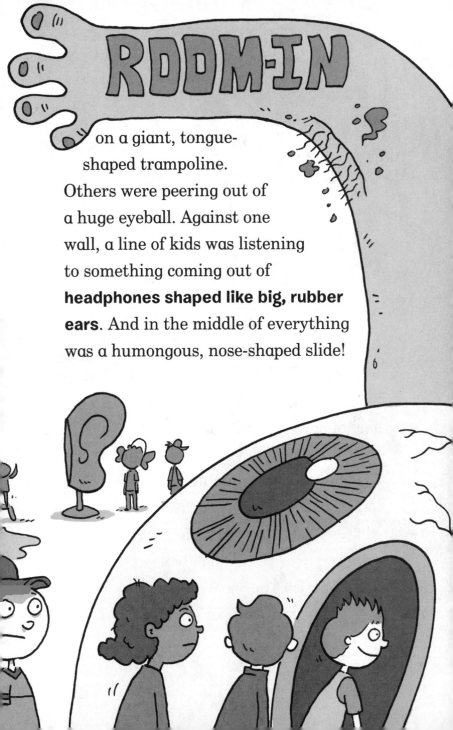

ROOM-IN

on a giant, tongue-shaped trampoline. Others were peering out of a huge eyeball. Against one wall, a line of kids was listening to something coming out of **headphones shaped like big, rubber ears**. And in the middle of everything was a humongous, nose-shaped slide!

There was only one place this could be. George had entered the Human Room-In!

Alex rushed over to the You Are Hear listening booths. He put ear-shaped headphones on and looked like he was bopping up and down to some kind of music. **That looked like fun.** But before George could go over to Alex, Sage called him over.

"Georgie, come here," Sage said. She was standing near the eyeball beneath a sign that read: Do You See What I See?

"Is this a princess or an old witch?" she

asked as she pointed to a poster on the wall.

George looked at the picture. If he squinted his eyes, he saw a young princess. But if he focused really hard on the princess's chin, it became an old lady's giant nose.

"I'm not sure," George said. **He squinted a little harder** to see if he could tell.

"That's why it's called an optical illusion," a museum worker named Meg told him. "You aren't sure what you see. Maybe it's a picture of both!"

"Hey, George, check this out!" Alex shouted suddenly.

George turned around. Alex had left the hearing station. Now he was climbing up on the big, red, tongue-shaped trampoline. That was **the taste station**. George walked over for a closer look.

The trampoline was covered with bumps. A museum guard was explaining that they were supposed to be taste buds. The words *sweet, sour, salty,* and *bitter* were written on the tongue. Right now, Alex was jumping on the front of the tongue trampoline, right on top of the word *sweet*.

"Come on!" Alex called to George.

No way. George
was not getting on
any trampoline.
Not even a cool one
that looked like a
tongue with taste
buds. The last
time he'd been on
a trampoline, he'd
jumped so high
his underwear got
caught on a tree
branch. Man, that
was **the world's
worst wedgie**. His rear
end hurt just thinking
about it.

Instead, George walked over to the
table where Chris and Julianna were
standing. The sign on the table read:
PLEASE TOUCH . . . IF YOU DARE.

There were round holes in the table; you were supposed to stick your hands in them. That way you could feel without seeing **what was lurking underneath the tabletop** in buckets.

"Uh, what's in there?" Chris exclaimed. He yanked his hand out quickly.

That got George's attention.

"Stick your hand in," Julianna told him.

George stuck his hand into the hole. *Oooh.* "Yikes!" he exclaimed. He pulled his hand out.

"Feels like teeth, doesn't it?" a security guard named Don asked him.

George nodded. "Wet teeth. Like ones that just came out of someone's mouth. **I think one of them tried to bite me.**"

"I doubt it," Don said.

"Why?" George asked him.

"Because corn kernels don't bite," Don told him. He pulled out a few kernels to show George.

"I was so sure it was teeth," George said. It was disappointing. Teeth would have been **so much cooler**.

"Don't feel bad," Chris said. "I was sure I was holding an eyeball. But it turned out to be just **a peeled, wet grape**."

"Your senses can play tricks on you," Don said with a smile.

Alex walked over to where George, Julianna, and Chris were standing. He looked up at Don. "Can I ask you something?" Alex asked him.

"That's why I'm here," Don said.

"Does gum really stay in your stomach for seven years if you swallow it?" Alex asked.

Don shook his head. "Nope. That's a myth. You actually don't digest gum at all. After you swallow it, it slides right through you and comes out in **your waste product**."

George laughed. He knew what that meant. "I'm all for helping you find already been chewed gum, dude," he told Alex. "But when it comes to already been pooped gum, you're on your own."

"I'll pass on that, too," Alex said. "No ABC gum for me!"

Just
then,
out of the
corner of his eye,
George spotted
Louie. He was climbing
a tall ladder. The ladder led
up to the very top of a giant nose.
Max and Mike were right behind
him.

"The nose slide is really fun,"
Don told the kids. "You follow
the path of a sneeze as you slide
through the nose. And every now
and then a new smell gets blasted

into the nostrils!"

George laughed. "I guess that makes Louie a giant booger!" he said as he watched Louie disappear into the giant nose.

"Max and Mike, too," Chris added. **"That sure is a runny nose!"**

George started laughing. He really wanted to check the slide out. But George stood right where he was and frowned.

Something was happening to him. And it wasn't funny at all!

Chapter 8

Bing-bong! Ping-pong! Bing-bong!
The magical super burp was back.
And it wanted out. NOW!

Boing-bing-boing! The bubbles
were bouncing all around now. Up over
George's kidneys and around his liver.
Ping-pong-ping! **The bubbles danced
their way into George's throat.** They
were headed straight for his lips.

George tapped his belly. He rubbed
his head. He tried to call out to Alex.
But Alex was staring at all the optical
illusions.

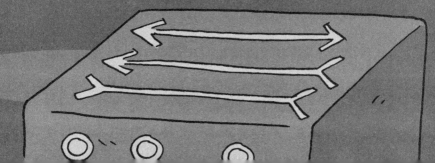

Unfortunately, the super burp was no illusion. It was **the real deal**. And it was on its way out.

George shut his mouth tight. He spun around in circles, trying to force the burp back down like water in a drain.

But the burp was strong. And it was mad that George had beaten it last time. No way was it losing again.

Bing . . . bong . . .

George let out a massive, mega burp! **The loudest burp in the history of burpdom!**

Everyone in the Human Room-In stopped what they were doing. Even the kids with the ear headphones on. They stared at George.

George opened his mouth to say "excuse me." But that's not what came out at all. Instead, George started dancing his way over to the giant nose and singing.

"It's the booger boogie! Everybody do the booger boogie," he sang out. **His rear end wiggled.** "Booger boogie!"

"What is that boy doing?" Meg asked Don.

"I think it's called the booger boogie,"
Don told her.

"Come on!" George's mouth shouted.
"Everybody join in!" His finger shot up
into his nose and wiggled all around.
"Everybody's doing it, doing it, doing
it. Everybody's chewing it, chewing it,
chewing it. Thinking it's candy, but it's
snot!" George's mouth sang out. He could

see Alex trying to rush over to help. But his path was blocked by a **bunch of kids all trying to do the booger boogie with George**.

"George!" Mrs. Kelly warned. "We're at a museum. That song is not appropriate."

"Georgie, you're so funny!" Sage giggled.

"Do the booger boogie!" Chris called out from the top of the giant nose slide. Then he slid down to the ground.

"Do the booger boogie!" Julianna sang from the tongue trampoline.

Max and Mike started to do their own booger boogie. But one look from Louie stopped them cold.

George's feet ran up the giant nose slide. His head poked its way up into one of the giant nostrils.

And then his body started climbing in.

"George!" Mrs. Kelly scolded. "You're not supposed to climb up into the slide. You're supposed to slide down."

But George's body scrambled farther up into the nostril. And then . . .

Whoosh! George felt something pop in the bottom of his belly. It was as if someone had busted a balloon down there. The super burp was gone. But George was still inside the giant nose. And he couldn't get out.

He wiggled to the left. He wiggled to the right. He sucked in his belly. But he was still jammed tight.

"Help! I'm stuck in a giant nostril!" he shouted.

"Ha-ha, kid. Very funny. Now come on out of there," a guard said.

But George wasn't kidding. He was really stuck. His legs were hanging out from the bottom of the giant nose like two long strands of boogers. Well, boogers with sneakers on the ends of them.

Inside the nostril, **tiny, wiry hair things** stuck out all over the place. Again, George tried to twist and wiggle free. But he was

still stuck. Even worse, those wiry hair
things were tickling his face and arms.

"Cut it out," George shouted. He kicked
his legs up and down. "That tickles."

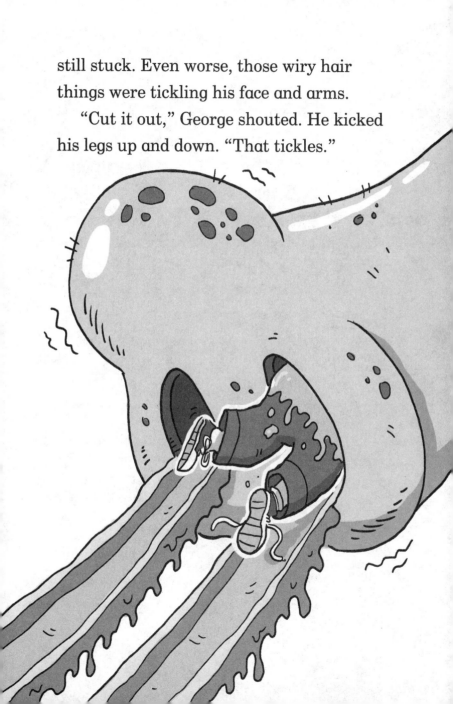

Just then George heard someone outside. It sounded like Louie. "George is freaking out again. I'm sure glad he didn't do this in the Farley Family Fungus Room. You can't freak out around fungus!"

Poof! Just then a blast of air poured into the giant nostril. **Spicy pizza smell filled the whole nose.**

Poof! Another blast of air poured into the nostril. This one didn't smell like pizza. It smelled like stinky gym shoes. Ugh. George felt like **he wanted to puke**.

"Get me out of here!" George shouted again.

"Somebody do something!" Mrs. Kelly called over to the museum workers.

Suddenly George felt someone yanking at his feet.

"George, can you hear me?" George

recognized that voice. It was Alex.

"Yes," George called back to him.

"Okay, try to wiggle yourself down while I pull," Alex said.

George wiggled and jiggled.

Alex pulled and yanked. But George didn't go anywhere.

"I know how to get him out!" Julianna shouted. She hurried to the top of the nose and slid down the nostril. She flew through the tiny nose hairs at top speed—and stopped short when her sneakers hit George's head.

"Ouch!" George shouted. "What are you doing?"

"Trying to get you out of here," Julianna said.

"Well, now we're both stuck." George groaned.

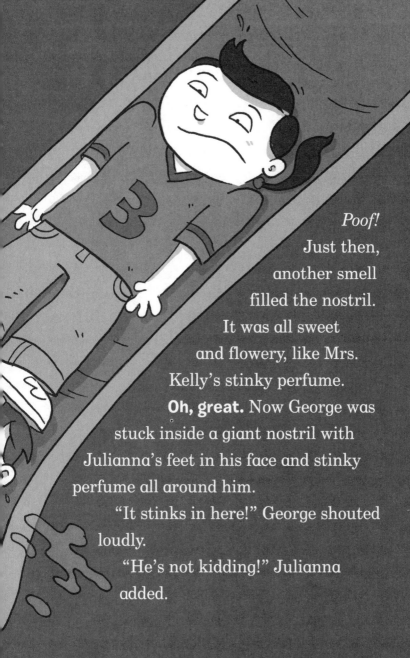

Poof!
Just then,
another smell
filled the nostril.
It was all sweet
and flowery, like Mrs.
Kelly's stinky perfume.
Oh, great. Now George was
stuck inside a giant nostril with
Julianna's feet in his face and stinky
perfume all around him.

"It stinks in here!" George shouted
loudly.

"He's not kidding!" Julianna
added.

"Chris, come help me pull George's legs," Alex said. "You grab one. I'll grab the other."

"Whoa!" George shouted as he got yanked out of the nostril and landed with **a thud**—right on top of Chris and Alex.

"Yikes!" Julianna screamed as she slid out and landed on George.

George poked his head out from the people pile. "Thanks, guys," he told Chris, Julianna, and Alex. "I didn't think I was ever getting out of there."

Louie walked over to George. "So was that the weirdest thing that ever happened to you?"

George picked himself up. "Um, I don't know. Lots of weird stuff happens to me. **Like this one time at my old school** . . ." George was about to tell Louie about the time he got a purple jelly bean stuck up his nose. But he didn't get the chance.

"Yessss!" Louie shouted. He pumped his fist in the air. "You said it! I heard you! You said 'at my old school'!"

"He definitely said it," Max agreed.

"I heard you," Mike agreed. "*Everybody* heard you."

George looked at his friends. Chris, Julianna, and Alex were all nodding sadly.

Oh, man! George couldn't believe it. **He'd totally forgotten about the bet.** And now he was going to be Louie's servant for a whole day. Was that worse than being stuck in a giant nose?

George decided it was a toss-up.

Chapter 9

"Louie, you're up next," Julianna called from the pitcher's mound during gym class the next morning.

Louie walked over to home plate. "Come on, George," he called over to the bench.

"What?" George asked him. "I'm not up next."

"But you're my servant for the day," Louie explained. "So after I hit the ball, you're going to do all the running." He glared at George. "**And you'd better be fast.** I don't want our team to lose just because you run slowly."

George frowned. Louie was making him crazy. Already he'd made George hang up his coat in the coat closet, take all his really heavy books back to the library, and clean up his table after art class. Now he was making him run for him. **This was getting ridiculous.**

"Mr. Trainer will never go for this," George told Louie.

"Wanna bet?" Louie asked. He turned toward the first-base line where Mr. Trainer, the gym teacher, was standing. "Is it okay if George pinch-runs for me today?" he asked. "My foot hurts."

"Sure, Louie," Mr. Trainer said. "Just hit the ball."

Louie picked up the bat. Then he put it down again. "I call time-out."

"What's wrong?" Mr. Trainer asked.

"My shoelace is untied," Louie explained. He looked at George. **"Tie my lace, Servant for the Day."**

Grrr and double grrr.

Louie was really being

a jerk about this. Not that it was all that surprising. Louie was pretty much a jerk about everything.

George bent down and began to tie Louie's shoe.

"No, not that way," Louie said. "I always tie my shoes with the two bunny ears."

Triple grrr.

As soon as his shoelace was tied, Louie picked up his bat and got ready for Julianna's pitch.

She wound up her arm
and let the ball fly toward
the plate.

"Miss, miss, miss," George wished
quietly under his breath. He didn't want
his team to lose, but he didn't want
Louie to get a good
hit, either.

SMACK! Louie
hit **a long drive**
into left field.

"Run!" Louie
ordered George.

George ran. He touched first base, made it to second, rounded third, and then . . . Julianna threw the ball toward home plate.

"Slide!" Louie shouted.

Rrripppp.

That was the sound of George's new
jeans ripping as he slid toward home
plate. Oh, man, **his mom was going to
be so mad**.

"Safe!" Mr. Trainer shouted. "Good
slide, George. You won the game for your
team!"

"No, *I* won the game," Louie said.
"He was pinch-running for me. It was
my home run!"

"Either way, your team won."
Mr. Trainer looked at his watch. "Let's get inside, gang. Lunch is waiting."

"You'd better wash your hands before lunch," Louie told George. "I'm going to want you to cut my meat loaf for me. And you're a mess."

George rolled his eyes. This was the **longest day in history**. The only good thing was that, for once, the magic super burp had kept its distance.

Alex walked over to George. "I have a pair of sweatpants in my backpack," he told him. "They might fit you."

"Thanks." George smiled. He was glad Alex didn't mind having a best friend who burped.

"Oh, and I have another idea for getting rid of the super burp," Alex told him. **"Have you tried an onion milk shake?"**

George gave Alex a funny look. "That sounds disgusting."

"But onions help fight gas," Alex said. "And

milk coats your stomach, too. It might be worth a try."

George shrugged. Why not? Although George had a feeling that sooner or later, **the burp would be back**. And when it returned, it was sure to bring trouble. Ba-a-ad trouble!

About the Author

Nancy Krulik is the author of more than 150 books for children and young adults including three *New York Times* best sellers and the popular Katie Kazoo, Switcheroo books. She lives in New York City with her family, and many of George Brown's escapades are based on things her own kids have done. (No one delivers a good burp quite like Nancy's son, Ian!) Nancy's favorite thing to do is laugh, which comes in pretty handy when you're trying to write funny books!

About the Illustrator

Aaron Blecha was raised by a school of giant squid in Wisconsin and now lives with his family by the English seaside. He works as an artist designing toys, animating cartoons, and illustrating books, including the Zombiekins and The Rotten Adventures of Zachary Ruthless series. You can enjoy more of his weird creations at www.monstersquid.com.